COLLECTION MANAGEMENT

SUPERMAN ™

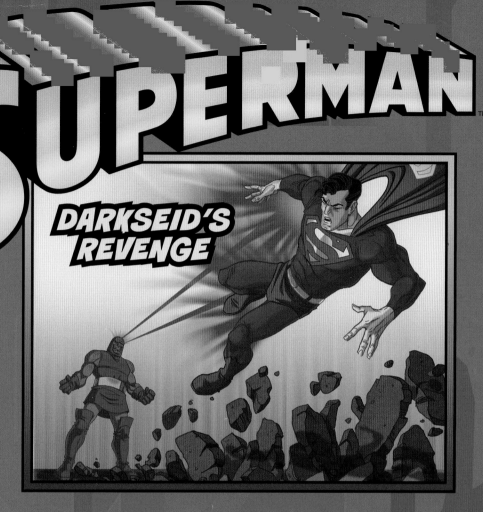

DARKSEID'S REVENGE

BY **DEVAN APTEKAR**
ILLUSTRATED BY **STEVEN E. GORDON**
DIGITAL COLORS BY **ERIC A. GORDON**

SUPERMAN created by Jerry Siegel and Joe Shuster
BATMAN created by Bob Kane
WONDER WOMAN created by William Moulton Marston

HARPER FESTIVAL
An Imprint of HarperCollinsPublishers

HarperFestival is an imprint of HarperCollins Publishers.

Superman: Darkseid's Revenge
Copyright © 2012 DC Comics.
SUPERMAN, BATMAN, WONDER WOMAN, and all related characters and elements
are trademarks of and © DC Comics. (s12)
HARP2511
Manufactured in China.
No part of this book may be used or reproduced in any manner whatsoever without written
permission except in the case of brief quotations embodied in critical articles and reviews.
For information address HarperCollins Children's Books,
a division of HarperCollins Publishers, 10 East 53rd Street, New York, NY 10022.
www.harpercollinschildrens.com

Library of Congress catalog card number: 2011929314
ISBN 978-0-06-188533-4
Book design by John Sazaklis
12 13 14 15 16   SCP   10 9 8 7 6 5 4 3 2 1
❖
First Edition

JJ Fic

THE SUPER HEROES AND VILLAINS IN THIS BOOK!

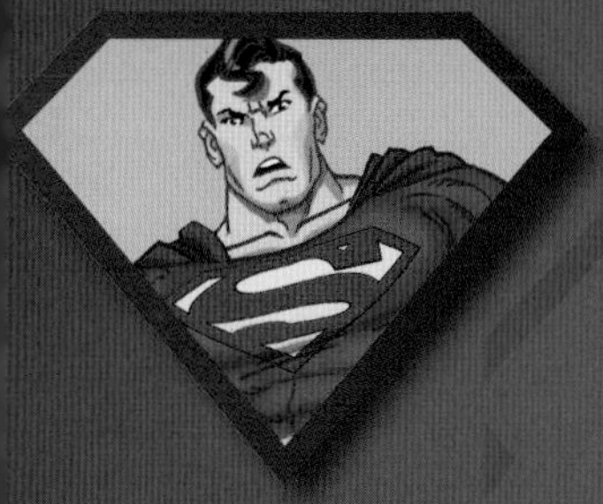

SUPERMAN

Sent to Earth from Krypton, Superman was raised as Clark Kent by small-town farmers and taught to value truth and justice. When not flying around to save the world with his super-strength, heat vision, and freezing breath, Clark is a reporter for Metropolis's newspaper, the *Daily Planet*.

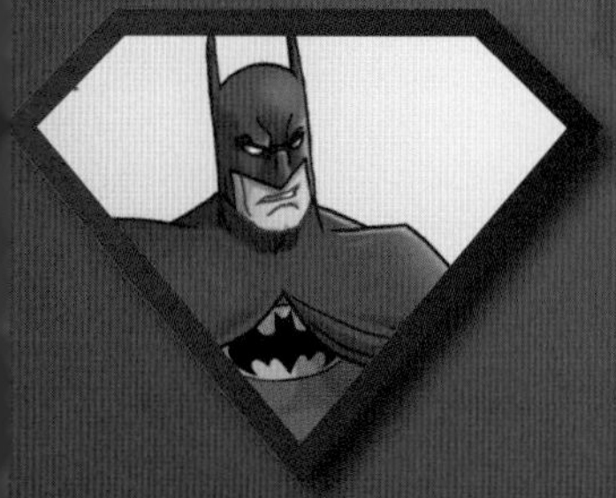

BATMAN

As a boy, the billionaire Bruce Wayne swore to avenge the deaths of his parents. He spent years mastering all forms of combat and creating an arsenal of cutting-edge equipment. He now fights crime in Gotham City as Batman.

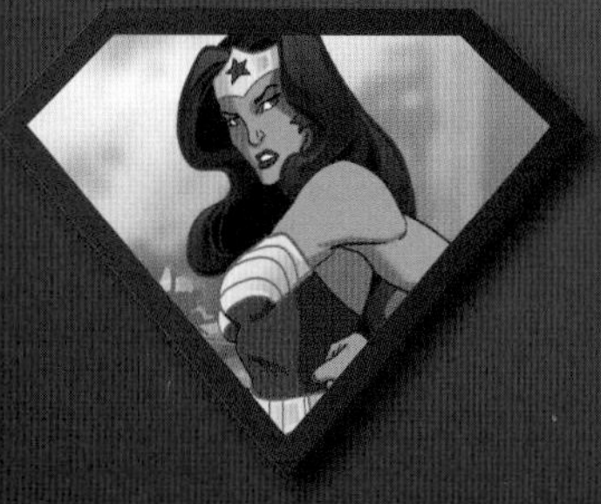

WONDER WOMAN

Born on Paradise Island, home of the Amazons, Wonder Woman was given the gifts of great wisdom, strength, beauty, and speed by the ancient Greek gods. Using her Invisible Jet, magic lasso, and unbreakable silver bracelets, she fights for peace and justice.

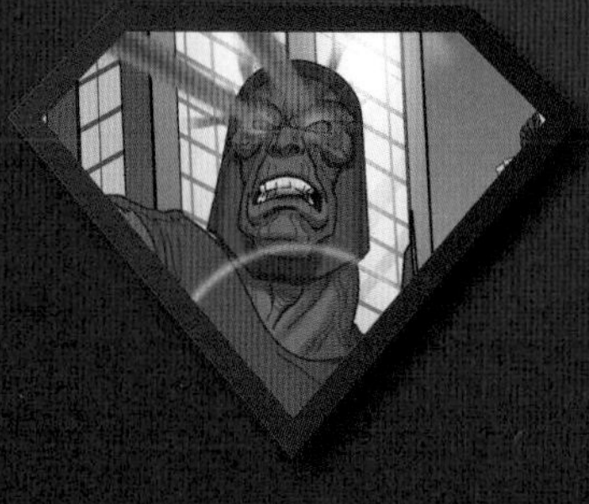

DARKSEID

Supreme ruler of the fiery planet Apokolips, Darkseid is determined to conquer the entire universe. Besides having immense strength and invulnerability, he is able to shoot Omega Beams from his eyes and can travel to different worlds and dimensions using a device known as a Mother Box.

It is another beautiful day in Metropolis. But high up in the Daily Planet building, someone is about to make a horrible discovery.

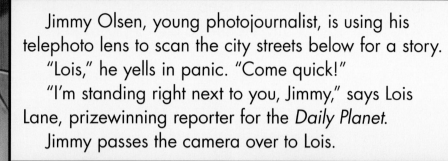

Jimmy Olsen, young photojournalist, is using his telephoto lens to scan the city streets below for a story.

"Lois," he yells in panic. "Come quick!"

"I'm standing right next to you, Jimmy," says Lois Lane, prizewinning reporter for the *Daily Planet*.

Jimmy passes the camera over to Lois.

"Darkseid." Lois gasps. "You keep snapping pictures. This story could wreck us all."

"Wait, Lois!" says Jimmy. He sees a blur of blue and red beside Darkseid. "He's here! Superman is here!"

"I just hope he can stop that fiend," says Lois. "Do we have any binoculars around here?

"Welcome, Kal-El, son of Krypton," murmurs Darkseid. His voice is low, but it echoes across downtown.

"Get out of Metropolis, Darkseid," says Superman. "You don't belong here. Go back to Apokolips now."

"Nor do you belong here, Kal-El," says Darkseid. "I'm tired of your misplaced pride in this ridiculous planet. You will destroy this city for me—TODAY!—while the earthlings watch in horror."

"Not a chance," says Superman, launching himself at Darkseid.

With a massive red blast, Darkseid releases Omega Beams from his eyes, sending Superman sprawling.

"I've modified my Omega Beams, son of Krypton. Feel how they wash through your brain," says Darkseid. "You serve *me* now."

"Say it," says Darkseid. "Life and hope are useless."

"Life and hope are useless," repeats Superman, stumbling to his feet.

"Now destroy this useless city," says Darkseid. "And mourn inside as you tear your adopted planet to shreds. Together we will rebuild it in Apokolips's image."

"Yes, my liege," says Superman.

Wonder Woman is soaring over the city in her Invisible Jet when a car comes hurtling past. She quickly locks it in her tractor beams so it won't fall.

"Superman? But why? How?"

As Wonder Woman dives toward the streets to protect Metropolis from its own protector, she sends a message to the greatest detective she knows.

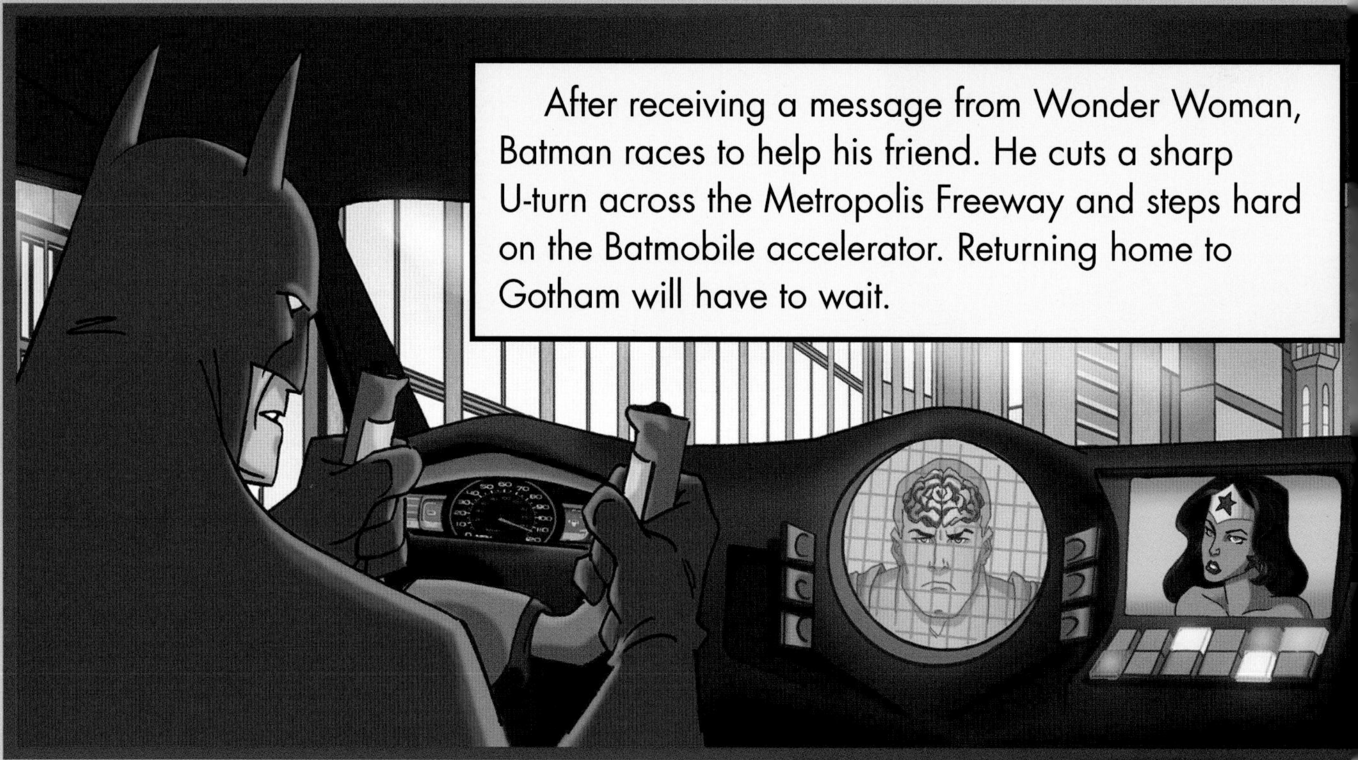
After receiving a message from Wonder Woman, Batman races to help his friend. He cuts a sharp U-turn across the Metropolis Freeway and steps hard on the Batmobile accelerator. Returning home to Gotham will have to wait.

He scans the city to find Superman and measures his brain waves. They don't match his normal brain signature. Batman quickly pulls up everything he knows about Darkseid as his vehicle roars toward downtown.

DARKSEID

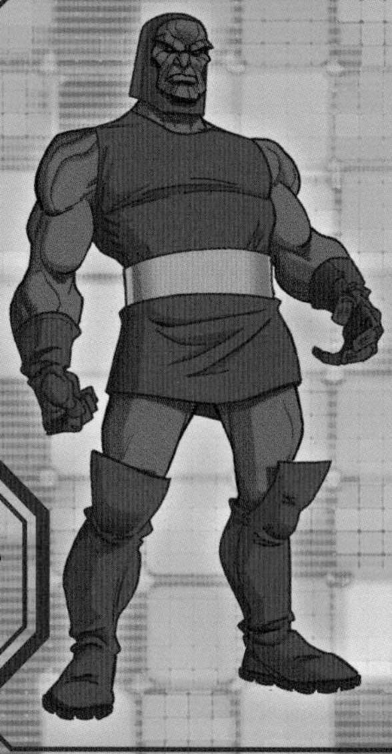

REAL NAME: UXAS

OCCUPATION: TYRANT

STATUS: VILLAIN

HEIGHT: 8FT 9IN

WEIGHT: 1,815 LBS

EYES: RED

HAIR: NONE

BASE: APOKOLIPS

ABILITIES: IMMENSE STRENGTH, NEAR INVULNERABILITY, OMEGA BEAM BLASTS, TRAVELS THROUGH TIME AND SPACE WITH USE OF MOTHER BOX DEVICE.

Wonder Woman is managing to keep people safe, but she is scrambling. She doesn't want to fight her friend. She clears the passengers off a bus before Superman grabs it, hurling the bus at the Daily Planet building. CRASH!

The crash jolts the building, making Jimmy Olsen drop his camera. Lois scoops it up and hands it right back. "Just keep snapping," she says.

Ten seconds later, the Batmobile screeches to a stop beside Wonder Woma "What took you so long?" she says.

Batman grunts in response. "Get your Lasso of Truth on him," he says. "He'll be vulnerable to the magic."

Wonder Woman shakes her head. "I've tried. He's too quick and there are too many people to save."

Wonder Woman and Batman try to grab their brainwashed friend, but he flies out of their grasp and blows them flat to the ground. Trees fall down around them.

Batman runs back toward Superman, but this time Darkseid pounds the ground between them. The shock waves send Batman flying back. "Sit, Dark Knight," says Darkseid. "Watch the hero destroy his city."

Superman rips the giant metal globe off the top of the Daily Planet building. He lifts it and slowly lowers himself, ready to throw it right through the steel-and-glass facade. Darkseid nods in approval.

Batman leaps into the air, assisted by Wonder Woman. At the peak of his leap, he throws Wonder Woman's magic lasso, pinning Superman's arms to his side. The massive globe tumbles toward the ground. People shriek and scatter, but Wonder Woman is there to catch it!

"I must destroy Earth and build a new Apokolips," says Superman. "Life and hope are useless."

"That's not who you are," says Batman. "Let Diana's rope bring you back to yourself. Darkseid is the one who's useless here."

Superman's vision begins to clear. He realizes he is looking right at the Daily Planet roof where Lois and Jimmy are staring back at him. "I'm sorry," he whispers.

Superman flies down to Wonder Woman and Batman and returns the lasso.

Darkseid chuckles. "Look at the destruction you have already wrought, Kal-El. There is more to come."

"No, Darkseid," says Superman. "My friends and I are saving lives today."

Darkseid lets loose his Omega Beams at all three heroes, but Superman acts just as fast. He counters with his own heat vision and the two blasts meet. Superman and Darkseid push closer, each trying to overpower the other.

Batman quickly flips a Batarang at Darkseid, pulling the Mother Box off his suit.

Darkseid is too distracted to notice the device he uses to travel dimensions has been taken.

Batman pulls the box and activates the Boom Tube that will teleport Darkseid across the universe to Apokolips.

"Back to where you came from, Darkseid," mutters Batman.

The heroes help rebuild Metropolis. It will take time to repair everything, but with hope and super heroes, anything is possible.